SELECTIONS FROM

THE ORIGINAL 1896
BOSTON COOKING-SCHOOL
COOK BOOK

FANNIE MERRITT FARMER

SELECTIONS FROM

THE ORIGINAL 1896 BOSTON COOKING-SCHOOL COOK BOOK

penguin books

PENGUIN BOOKS
Published by the Penguin Group
Penguin Books USA Inc., 375 Hudson Street,
New York, New York 10014, U.S.A.
Penguin Books Ltd, 27 Wrights Lane,
London W8 5TZ, England
Penguin Books Australia Ltd, Ringwood,
Victoria, Australia
Penguin Books Canada Ltd, 10 Alcorn Avenue,
Toronto, Ontario, Canada M4V 3B2
Penguin Books (N.Z.) Ltd, 182–190 Wairau Road,
Auckland 10, New Zealand

Penguin Books Ltd, Registered Offices:
Harmondsworth, Middlesex, England

Published in Penguin Books 1995

ISBN 0 14 60.0105 2

Printed in the United States of America

TO

MRS. WILLIAM B. SEWALL,

PRESIDENT OF THE
BOSTON COOKING-SCHOOL,
IN APPRECIATION OF HER HELPFUL ENCOURAGEMENT
AND UNTIRING EFFORTS IN PROMOTING THE WORK
OF SCIENTIFIC COOKERY, WHICH MEANS THE
ELEVATION OF THE HUMAN RACE,

THIS BOOK IS
AFFECTIONATELY DEDICATED

BY THE AUTHOR.

CONTENTS

PREFACE

"But for life the universe were nothing; and all that has life requires nourishment."

With the progress of knowledge the needs of the human body have not been forgotten. During the last decade much time has been given by scientists to the study of foods and their dietetic value, and it is a subject which rightfully should demand much consideration from all. I certainly feel that the time is not far distant when a knowledge of the principles of diet will be an essential part of one's education. Then mankind will eat to live, will be able to do better mental and physical work, and disease will be less frequent.

At the earnest solicitation of educators, pupils, and friends, I have been urged to prepare this book, and I trust it may be a help to many who need its aid. It is my wish that it may not only be looked upon as a compilation of tried and tested recipes, but that it may awaken an interest through its condensed scientific knowledge which will lead to deeper thought and broader study of what to eat.

—F. M. F.

TABLE OF MEASURES
AND WEIGHTS

2 cups butter (packed solidly)	= 1 pound.
2 " flour (pastry)	= 1 "
2 " granulated sugar	= 1 "
2⅔ " powdered sugar	= 1 "
3½ " confectioners' sugar	= 1 "
2⅔ " brown sugar	= 1 "
2⅔ " oatmeal	= 1 "
4¾ " rolled oats	= 1 "
2⅔ " granulated corn meal	= 1 "
4⅓ " rye meal	= 1 "
1⅞ " rice	= 1 "
4½ " Graham flour	= 1 "
3⅞ " entire wheat flour	= 1 "
4⅓ " coffee	= 1 "
2 " finely chopped meat	= 1 "
9 large eggs	= 1 "
1 square Baker's chocolate	= 1 ounce
⅓ cup almonds blanched and chopped	= 1 "

A few grains is less than one-eighth teaspoon.

3 teaspoons...= 1 tablespoon.

16 tablespoons ....= 1 cup.

2 tablespoons butter ....= 1 ounce.

4 tablespoons flour ....= 1 ounce.

TIME TABLES FOR COOKING

Boiling

ARTICLES	TIME	
	Hours	Minutes
Coffee		1 to 3
Eggs, soft cooked		6 to 8
" hard "		35 to 45
Mutton, leg	2 to 3	
Ham, weight 12 to 14 lbs.	4 to 5	
Corned Beef or Tongue	3 to 4	
Turkey, weight 9 lbs.	2 to 3	
Fowl, " 4 to 5 lbs.	2 to 3	
Chicken, " 3 lbs.	1 to 1¼	
Lobster		25 to 30
Cod and Haddock, weight 3 to 5 lbs.		20 to 30
Halibut, thick piece, " 2 to 3 lbs.		30
Bluefish and Bass, " 4 to 5 lbs.		40 to 45
Salmon, weight, 2 to 3 lbs.		30 to 35
Small Fish		6 to 10
Potatoes, white		20 to 30
" sweet		15 to 25
Asparagus		20 to 30
Peas		20 to 60
String Beans	1 to 2½	
Lima and other Shell Beans	1 to 1¼	

ARTICLES	TIME	
	Hours	Minutes
Beets, young		45
" old	3 to 4	
Cabbage		35 to 60
Oyster Plant		45 to 60
Turnips		30 to 45
Onions		45 to 60
Parsnips		30 to 45
Spinach		25 to 30
Green Corn		12 to 20
Cauliflower		20 to 25
Brussels Sprouts		15 to 20
Tomatoes, stewed		15 to 20
Rice		20 to 30
Macaroni		20 to 25

Broiling

Steak, one inch thick	4 to 6
" one and one-half inch thick	8 to 10
Lamb or Mutton Chops	6 to 8
" " " in paper cases	10
Quails or Squabs	8
" " in paper cases	10 to 12
Chickens	20

ARTICLES	TIME	
	Hours	Minutes
Shad, Bluefish, and Whitefish		15 to 20
Slices of Fish, Halibut, Salmon, and Swordfish		12 to 15
Small, thin Fish		5 to 8
Liver and Tripe		4 to 5

Baking

	Hours	Minutes
Bread (white loaf)		45 to 60
" (Graham loaf)		35 to 45
" (sticks)		10 to 15
Biscuits or Rolls (raised)		12 to 20
" (baking powder)		12 to 15
Gems		25 to 30
Muffins (raised)		30
" (baking powder)		20 to 25
Corn Cake (thin)		15 to 20
" (thick)		30 to 35
Gingerbread		20 to 30
Cookies		6 to 10
Sponge Cake		45 to 60
Cake (layer)		20 to 30
" (loaf)		40 to 60
" (pound)	1¼ to 1½	
" (fruit)	1¼ to 2	

ARTICLES	TIME	
	Hours	Minutes
Cake (wedding)..3		
or steam 2 hours and bake 1½		
Baked batter puddings.....................................35 to 45		
Bread puddings 1		
Tapioca or Rice Pudding 1		
Rice Pudding (poor man's)......................2 to 3		
Indian " ....2 to 3		
Plum " ....2 to 3		
Custard " ....30 to 45		
" (baked in cups) ....20 to 25		
Pies ....30 to 50		
Tarts ....15 to 20		
Patties ....20 to 25		
Vol-au-vent ....50 to 60		
Cheese Straws..8 to 10		
Scalloped Oysters ....25 to 30		
Scalloped dishes of cooked mixtures...............12 to 15		
Baked Beans ....6 to 8		
Braised Beef..3½ to 4½		
Beef, sirloin or rib, rare, weight 5 lbs............1		5
" " " " " 10 "...............1		30
" " " well done, weight 5 lbs...1		20
" " " " " 10 "................1		50
Beef, rump, rare, weight 10 lbs.....................1		35
" " well done, weight 10 lbs.............1		55

ARTICLES	TIME	
	Hours	Minutes
" (fillet)		20 to 30
Mutton (saddle)	1¼ to 1½	
Lamb (leg)	1¼ to 1¾	
" (forequarter)	1 to 1¼	
" (chops) in paper cases		15 to 20
Veal (leg)	3½ to 4	
" (loin)	2 to 3	
Pork (chine or sparerib)	3 to 3½	
Chicken, weight 3 to 4 lbs.	1 to 1½	
Turkey, weight 9 lbs.	2½ to 3	
Goose, weight 9 lbs.	2	
Duck (domestic)	1 to 1¼	
" (wild)		20 to 30
Grouse		25 to 30
Partridge		45 to 50
Pigeons (potted)	2	
Fish (thick), weight 3 to 4 lbs.		45 to 60
" (small)		20 to 30

Frying

ARTICLES	TIME	
	Hours	Minutes
Muffins, Fritters, and Doughnuts		3 to 5
Croquettes and Fishballs		1
Potatoes, raw		4 to 8
Breaded Chops		5 to 8
Fillets of Fish		4 to 6
Smelts, Trout, and other small Fish		3 to 5

NOTE—Length of time for cooking fish and meat does not depend so much on the number of pounds to be cooked as the extent of surface exposed to the heat.

SOUPS

Oyster Stew

1 quart oysters
4 cups scalded milk
¼ cup butter

½ tablespoon salt
⅛ teaspoon pepper

Clean oysters by placing in a colander and pouring over them three-fourths cup cold water. Carefully pick over oysters, reserve liquor, and heat it to boiling point; strain through double cheese cloth, add oysters, and cook until oysters are plump and edges begin to curl. Remove oysters with skimmer, and put in tureen with butter, salt, and pepper. Add oyster liquor, strained a second time, and milk. Serve with oyster crackers.

Black Bean Soup

1 pint black beans
2 quarts cold water
1 small onion
2 stalks celery, or
¼ teaspoon celery salt
½ tablespoon salt
⅛ teaspoon pepper

¼ teaspoon mustard
Few grains cayenne
3 tablespoons butter
1½ tablespoons flour
2 hard boiled eggs
1 lemon

Soak beans over night; in the morning drain and add cold water. Slice onion, and cook five minutes with half the butter, adding to beans, with celery stalks broken in pieces. Simmer three or four hours, or until beans are soft; add more water as water boils away. Rub through a sieve, reheat to the boiling point, and add salt, pepper, mustard, and cayenne well mixed. Bind with remaining butter and flour cooked together. Cut eggs in thin slices, and lemon in thin slices, removing seeds. Put in tureen, and strain the soup over them.

Split Pea Soup

1 cup dried split peas	3 tablespoons butter
2½ quarts cold water	2 tablespoons flour
1 pint milk	1½ teaspoons salt
½ onion	⅛ teaspoon pepper

Pick over peas and soak several hours, drain, add cold water and onion. Simmer three or four hours, or until soft; rub through a sieve. Add butter and flour cooked together, salt, and pepper. Dilute with milk, adding more if necessary. The water in which a ham has been cooked may be used; in such case omit salt.

Potato Soup

3 potatoes	1½ teaspoons salt
1 quart milk	¼ teaspoon celery salt
2 slices onion	⅛ teaspoon pepper
4 tablespoons butter	Few grains cayenne
2 tablespoons flour	1 teaspoon chopped parsley

Cook potatoes in boiling salted water; when soft, rub through a strainer. Scald milk with onion, remove onion, and add milk slowly to potatoes. Melt half the butter, add dry ingredients, stir until well mixed, then stir into boiling soup; cook one minute, strain, add remaining butter, and sprinkle with parsley.

Vegetable Soup

⅓ cup carrot
⅓ cup turnip
½ cup celery
1½ cups potato
½ onion

1 quart water
5 tablespoons butter
½ tablespoon finely chopped
   parsley
Salt and pepper

Wash and scrape a small carrot; cut in quarters lengthwise; cut quarters in thirds lengthwise; cut strips thus made in thin slices crosswise. Wash and pare half a turnip, and cut and slice same as carrot. Wash, pare, and cut potatoes in small pieces. Wash and scrape celery and cut in quarter-inch pieces. Prepare vegetables before measuring. Cut onion in thin slices. Mix vegetables (except potatoes), and cook ten minutes, in four tablespoons butter, stirring constantly. Add potatoes, cover, and cook two minutes. Add water, and boil one hour. Beat with spoon or fork to break vegetables. Add remaining butter and parsley. Season with salt and pepper.

Fish Chowder

4 lb. cod or haddock
6 cups potatoes cut in ¼ inch slices, or
4 cups potatoes cut in ¾ inch cubes
1 sliced onion

1½ inch cube fat salt pork
1 tablespoon salt
⅛ teaspoon pepper
3 tablespoons butter
4 cups scalded milk
8 common crackers

Order the fish skinned, but head and tail left on. Cut off head and tail and remove fish from backbone. Cut fish in two-inch pieces and set aside. Put head, tail, and backbone broken in pieces, in stewpan; add two cups cold water and bring slowly to boiling point; cook twenty minutes. Cut salt pork in small pieces and try out, add onion, and fry five minutes; strain fat into stewpan. Parboil potatoes five minutes in boiling water to cover; drain, and add potatoes to fat; then add two cups boiling water and cook five minutes. Add liquor drained from bones and fish; cover, and simmer ten minutes. Add milk, salt, pepper, butter, and crackers split and soaked in enough cold milk to moisten. Pilot bread is sometimes used in place of common crackers.

Clam Chowder

1 quart clams	1 tablespoon salt
4 cups potatoes cut in ¾ inch dice	⅛ teaspoon pepper
	4 tablespoons butter
1½ inch cube fat salt pork	4 cups scalded milk
1 sliced onion	8 common crackers

Clean and pick over clams, using one cup cold water; drain, reserve liquor, heat to boiling point, and strain. Chop finely hard part of clams; cut pork in small pieces and try out; add onion, fry five minutes, and strain into a stewpan. Parboil potatoes five minutes in boiling water to cover; drain and put a layer in bottom of stewpan, add chopped clams, sprinkle with salt and pepper, and dredge generously with flour; add remaining potatoes, again sprinkle with salt and pepper, dredge with flour, and add two and one-half cups boiling water. Cook ten minutes, add milk, soft part of clams, and butter; boil three minutes, and add crackers split and soaked in enough cold milk to moisten. Reheat clam water to boiling point, and thicken with one tablespoon butter and flour cooked together. Add to chowder just before serving.

The clam water has a tendency to cause the milk to separate, hence is added at the last.

ENTREES

Baked Halibut with Tomato Sauce

2 lbs. halibut	½ tablespoon sugar
2 cups tomatoes	3 tablespoons butter
1 cup water	3 tablespoons flour
1 slice onion	¾ teaspoon salt
3 cloves	⅛ teaspoon pepper

Cook twenty minutes tomatoes, water, onion, cloves, and sugar. Melt butter, add flour, and stir into hot mixture. Add salt and pepper, cook ten minutes, and strain. Clean fish, put in baking-pan, pour around half the sauce, and bake thirty-five minutes, basting often. Remove to hot platter, pour around remaining sauce, and garnish with parsley.

Halibut à la Poulette

A slice of halibut, weighing 1½ lbs.
¼ cup melted butter
⅛ teaspoon pepper
2 teaspoons lemon juice
Few drops onion juice
¼ teaspoon salt

Clean fish and cut in eight fillets. Add seasonings to melted butter, and put dish containing butter in saucepan of hot water to keep butter melted. Take up each fillet separately with a fork, dip in butter, roll, and fasten with a small wooden skewer. Put in shallow pan, dredge with flour, and bake twelve minutes in hot oven. Remove skewers, arrange on platter for serving, pour around one and one-half cups Béchamel Sauce, and garnish with yolks of two hard boiled eggs rubbed through a strainer, whites of hard boiled eggs cut in strips, lemon cut fan-shaped, and parsley.

Fried Smelts

Clean smelts, leaving on heads and tails. Sprinkle with salt and pepper, dip in flour, egg, and crumbs, and fry three to four minutes in deep fat. As soon as smelts are put into fat, remove fat to back of range so that they may not become too brown before cooked through. Arrange on hot platter, garnish with parsley, lemon, and fried gelatine. Serve with Sauce Tartare.

Soft-shell Crabs

Clean crabs, sprinkle with salt and pepper, dip in crumbs, egg, and crumbs, fry in deep fat, and drain. Being light they will rise to top of fat, and should be turned while frying. Soft-shell crabs are usually fried.

To Clean a Crab. Lift and fold back the tapering points which are found on each side of the back shell, and remove spongy substance that lies under them. Turn crab on its back, and with a pointed knife remove the small piece at lower part of shell, which terminates in a point; this is called the apron.

Oyster Fricassee

1 pint oysters
Milk or cream
2 tablespoons butter
2 tablespoons flour
¼ teaspoon salt

Few grains cayenne
1 teaspoon finely chopped
 parsley
1 egg

Clean oysters, heat oyster liquor to boiling point and strain through double thickness of cheese cloth; add oysters to liquor and cook until plump. Remove oysters with skimmer and add enough cream to liquor to make a cupful. Melt butter, add flour, and pour on gradually hot liquid; add salt, cayenne, parsley, oysters, and egg slightly beaten.

Scalloped Oysters

1 pint oysters
4 tablespoons oyster liquor
2 tablespoons milk or cream
½ cup stale bread crumbs

1 cup cracker crumbs
½ cup melted butter
Salt
Pepper

Mix bread and cracker crumbs, and stir in butter. Put a thin layer in bottom of a buttered shallow baking-dish, cover with oysters, and sprinkle with salt and pepper; add one-half each of oyster liquor and cream. Repeat, and cover top with remaining crumbs. Bake thirty minutes in hot oven. Never allow more than two layers of oysters for Scalloped Oysters; if three layers are used, the middle layer will be underdone, while others are properly cooked. A sprinkling of mace or grated nutmeg to each layer is considered by many an improvement. Sherry wine may be used in place of cream.

Stuffed Lobster à la Béchamel

2 lb. lobster	Few grains cayenne
1½ cups milk	Slight grating nutmeg
Bit of bay leaf	1 teaspoon chopped parsley
3 tablespoons butter	1 teaspoon lemon juice
3 tablespoons flour	Yolks 2 eggs
½ teaspoon salt	½ cup buttered crumbs

Remove lobster meat from shell and cut in dice. Scald milk with bay leaf, remove bay leaf and make a White Sauce of butter, flour, and milk; add salt, cayenne, nutmeg, parsley, yolks of eggs slightly beaten, and lemon juice. Add lobster dice, refill shells, cover with buttered crumbs, and bake until crumbs are brown. One-half chicken stock and one-half cream may be used for sauce if a richer dish is desired.

Shrimps à la Newburg

1 pint shrimps	1 teaspoon flour
3 tablespoons butter	½ cup cream
½ teaspoon salt	Yolks 2 eggs
Few grains cayenne	2 tablespoons sherry wine
1 teaspoon lemon juice	

Clean shrimps and cook three minutes in two tablespoons butter. Add salt, cayenne, and lemon juice, and cook one minute. Remove shrimps, and put remaining butter in chafing-dish, add flour and cream; when thickened, add yolks of eggs slightly beaten, shrimps, and wine. Serve with toast.

Irish Stew with Dumplings

Wipe and cut in pieces three pounds lamb from the fore-quarter. Put in kettle, cover with boiling water, and cook slowly two hours or until tender. After cooking one hour, add one-half cup each carrot and turnip cut in one-half inch cubes, and one onion cut in slices. Fifteen minutes before serving add four cups potatoes cut in one-fourth inch slices, previously parboiled five minutes in boiling water. Thicken with one-fourth cup flour, diluted with enough cold water to form a thin smooth paste. Season with salt and pepper, serve with Dumplings.

Dumplings

2 cups flour
4 teaspoons baking powder
½ teaspoon salt

2 teaspoons butter
¾ cup milk

Mix and sift dry ingredients. Work in butter with tips of fingers, add milk gradually, using a knife for mixing. Toss on a floured board, pat, and roll out to one-half inch in thickness. Shape with biscuit cutter, first dipped in flour. Place closely together in a buttered steamer, put over kettle of boiling water, cover closely, and steam twelve minutes. A perforated tin pie plate may be used in place of steamer. A little more milk may be used in the mixture, when it may be taken up by spoonfuls, dropped and cooked on top of stew. In this case some of the liquid must be removed, that dumplings may rest on meat and potato, and not settle into liquid.

Chicken Curry

3 lb. chicken	1 tablespoon curry powder
⅓ cup butter	2 teaspoons salt
2 onions	1 teaspoon vinegar

Clean, dress, and cut chicken in pieces for serving. Put butter in a hot frying-pan, add chicken, and cook ten minutes; then add liver and gizzard and cook ten minutes longer. Cut onions in thin slices, and add to chicken with curry powder and salt. Add enough boiling water to cover, and simmer until chicken is tender. Remove chicken; strain and thicken liquor with flour diluted with enough cold water to pour easily. Pour gravy over chicken, and serve with a border of rice.

Welsh Rarebit I

1 tablespoon butter
1 teaspoon corn-starch
½ cup thin cream
½ lb. mild soft cheese cut
   in small pieces

¼ teaspoon salt
¼ teaspoon mustard
Few grains cayenne
Toast or zephyrettes

Melt butter, add corn-starch, stir until well mixed, then add cream gradually and cook two minutes. Add cheese, and stir until cheese is melted. Season, and serve on zephyrettes or bread toasted on one side, rarebit being poured over untoasted side.

Welsh Rarebit II

1 tablespoon butter
½ lb. mild soft cheese cut
   in small pieces
¼ teaspoon salt
¼ teaspoon mustard

Few grains cayenne
⅓ to ½ cup ale or lager beer
1 egg

Put butter in chafing-dish, and when melted, add cheese and seasonings; as cheese melts, add ale gradually; then egg slightly beaten. Serve as Welsh Rarebit I.

English Monkey

1 cup stale bread crumbs	1 egg
1 cup milk	½ teaspoon salt
1 tablespoon butter	Few grains cayenne
½ cup soft mild cheese cut in small pieces	

Soak bread crumbs fifteen minutes in milk. Melt butter, add cheese, and when cheese has melted, add soaked crumbs, egg slightly beaten, and seasonings. Cook three minutes, and pour over toasted crackers.

VEGETABLES

Boiled Artichokes

Cut off stem close to leaves, remove outside bottom leaves, trim artichoke, cut off one inch from top of leaves, and with a sharp knife remove choke; then tie artichoke with a string to keep its shape. Soak one-half hour in cold water. Drain, and cook thirty to forty-five minutes in boiling, salted, acidulated water. Remove from water, place upside down to drain, then take off string. Serve with Béchamel or Hollandaise Sauce. Boiled Artichokes often constitute a course at dinner. Leaves are drawn out separately with fingers, dipped in sauce, and fleshy ends only eaten, although the bottom is edible. Artichokes may be cut in quarters, cooked, drained, and served with Sauce Béarnaise. When prepared in this way they are served with mutton.

Boiled Asparagus

Cut off lower parts of stalks as far down as they will snap, untie bunches, wash, remove scales, and retie. Cook in boiling salted water fifteen minutes or until soft, leaving tips out of water first ten minutes. Drain, remove string, and spread with soft butter, allowing one and one-half tablespoons butter to each bunch asparagus. Asparagus is often broken in inch pieces for boiling, cooking tips a shorter time than stalks.

Boiled Beets

Wash, and cook whole in boiling water until soft; time required being from one to four hours. Old beets will never be tender, no matter how long they may be cooked. Drain and put in cold water, that skins may be easily removed. Serve cut in quarters or slices.

Sugared Beets

4 hot boiled beets   1½ tablespoons sugar
3 tablespoons butter   ½ teaspoon salt

Cut beets in one-fourth inch slices, add butter, sugar, and salt; reheat for serving.

Creamed Cauliflower

Remove leaves, cut off stalk, and soak thirty minutes (head down) in cold water to cover. Cook (head up) twenty minutes or until soft in boiling salted water; drain, separate flowerets, and reheat in one and one-half cups White Sauce.

White Sauce

2 tablespoons butter   ¼ teaspoon salt
2 tablespoons flour   Few grains pepper
1 cup milk

Put butter in saucepan, stir until melted and bubbling; add flour mixed with seasonings, and stir until thoroughly blended. Pour on gradually the milk, adding about one-third at a time, stirring until well mixed, then beating until smooth and glossy. If a wire whisk is used, all the milk may be added at once; and although more quickly made if milk is scalded, it is not necessary.

Corn Oysters

Grate raw corn from cobs. To one cup pulp add one well beaten egg, one-fourth cup flour, and season highly with salt and pepper. Drop by spoonfuls and fry in deep fat, or cook on a hot, well greased griddle. They should be made about the size of large oysters.

Chestnut Purée

Remove shells from chestnuts, cook until soft in boiling salted water; drain, mash, moisten with scalded milk; season with salt and pepper, and beat until light. Chestnuts are often boiled, riced, and piled lightly in centre of dish, then surrounded by meat.

Stuffed Egg-plant

Cook egg-plant fifteen minutes in boiling salted water to cover. Cut a slice from top and with a spoon remove pulp, taking care not to work too closely to skin. Chop pulp, and add one cup soft stale bread crumbs. Melt two tablespoons butter, add one-half tablespoon finely chopped onion, and cook five minutes; or try out three slices of bacon, using bacon fat in place of butter. Add to chopped pulp and bread, season with salt and pepper, and if necessary moisten with a little stock or water; cook five minutes, cool slightly, and add one beaten egg. Refill egg-plant, cover with buttered bread crumbs, and bake twenty-five minutes in a hot oven.

Baked Mushrooms in Cream

Wash twelve large mushrooms. Remove stems, and peel caps. Put in a shallow buttered pan, cap side up. Sprinkle with salt and pepper, and dot over with butter; add two-thirds cup cream. Bake ten minutes in a hot oven. Place on pieces of dry toast, and pour over them cream remaining in pan.

Stuffed Onions

Remove skins from onions, and parboil ten minutes in boiling salted water to cover. Turn upside down to cool, and remove part of centres. Fill cavities with equal parts of finely chopped cooked chicken, stale soft bread crumbs, and finely chopped onion which was removed, seasoned with salt and pepper, and moistened with cream or melted butter. Place in buttered shallow baking-pan, sprinkle with buttered crumbs, and bake in a moderate oven until onions are soft.

Parsnip Fritters

Wash parsnips and cook forty-five minutes in boiling salted water. Drain, plunge into cold water, when skins will be found to slip off easily. Mash, season with butter, salt, and pepper, shape in small flat round cakes, roll in flour, and sauté in butter.

Stuffed Peppers

6 green peppers
¾ cup hot steamed rice
½ cup cold cooked meat cut in small dice
1 tablespoon melted butter
⅓ cup tomatoes stewed and strained
Few drops onion juice
Salt and pepper

Cut off pieces from stem ends of peppers. Remove seeds and partitions; parboil eight minutes. Fill with rice, meat, tomatoes, and butter, well mixed, and seasoned with onion juice, salt, and pepper. Place in a pan, add one and one-half cups water or stock, and bake forty-five minutes in a moderate oven.

Potato Croquettes

2 cups hot riced potatoes
2 tablespoons butter
½ teaspoon salt
⅛ teaspoon pepper
¼ teaspoon celery salt

Few drops onion juice
Yolk 1 egg
1 teaspoon finely chopped
    parsley

Mix ingredients in order given, and beat thoroughly. Shape, dip in crumbs, egg, and crumbs again, fry one minute in deep fat, and drain on brown paper. Croquettes are shaped in a variety of forms. The most common way is to first form a smooth ball by rolling one rounding tablespoon mixture between hands. Then roll on a board until of desired length.

Glazed Sweet Potatoes

Wash and pare six medium-sized potatoes. Cook ten minutes in boiling salted water. Drain, cut in halves lengthwise, and put in a buttered pan. Make a syrup by boiling three minutes one-half cup sugar and four tablespoons water; add one table-spoon butter. Brush potatoes with syrup and bake until brown, basting with remaining syrup.

Devilled Tomatoes

3 tomatoes	1 teaspoon mustard
Salt and pepper	¼ teaspoon salt
Flour	Few grains cayenne
Butter for sautéing	Yolk 1 hard boiled egg
4 tablespoons butter	1 egg
2 teaspoons powdered sugar	2 tablespoons vinegar

Wipe, peel, and cut tomatoes in slices. Sprinkle with salt and pepper, dredge with flour, and sauté in butter. Place on a hot platter and pour over the dressing made by creaming the butter, adding dry ingredients, yolk of egg rubbed to a paste, egg beaten slightly, and vinegar, then cooking over hot water, stirring constantly until it thickens.

DESSERTS

Rice Pudding

5 cups milk
⅓ cup rice
½ teaspoon salt

⅓ cup sugar
Grated rind ½ lemon

Wash rice, mix ingredients, and pour into buttered pudding-dish; bake three hours in very slow oven, stirring three times during first hour of baking to prevent rice from settling.

Bread Pudding

2 cups stale bread crumbs
1 quart scalded milk
⅓ cup sugar
2 tablespoons melted butter

2 eggs
½ teaspoon salt
1 teaspoon vanilla or
¼ teaspoon spice

Soak bread crumbs in milk, set aside until cool; add sugar, butter, eggs slightly beaten, salt, and flavoring; bake one hour in buttered pudding-dish in slow oven. In preparing bread crumbs for puddings avoid using outside crusts. With a coarse grater there need be but little waste.

Charlotte Russe

¼ box gelatine or
1¼ tablespoons granulated
   gelatine
¼ cup cold water
⅓ cup scalded cream

⅓ cup powdered sugar
Whip from 3½ cups thin
   cream
1½ teaspoons vanilla
6 lady fingers

Soak gelatine in cold water, dissolve in scalded cream, strain into a bowl, and add sugar and vanilla. Set bowl in pan of ice water and stir constantly until it begins to thicken, then fold in whip from cream, adding one-third at a time. Should gelatine mixture become too thick, melt over hot water, and again cool before adding whip. Trim ends and sides of lady fingers, place around inside of a mould, crust side out, one-half inch apart. Turn in mixture, spread evenly, and chill. Serve on glass dish and garnish with cubes of Wine Jelly. Charlotte Russe is sometimes made in individual moulds; these are often garnished on top with some of mixture forced through a pastry bag and tube. Individual moulds are frequently lined with thin slices of sponge cake cut to fit moulds.

Soft Molasses Gingerbread

1 cup molasses	1 egg
⅓ cup butter	2 cups flour
1¾ teaspoons soda	2 teaspoons ginger
½ cup sour milk	½ teaspoon salt

Put butter and molasses in saucepan and cook until boiling point is reached. Remove from fire, add soda, and beat vigorously. Then add milk, egg well beaten, and remaining ingredients mixed and sifted. Bake fifteen minutes in buttered small tin pans, having pans two-thirds filled with mixture.

Molasses Cookies

1 cup molasses
½ cup shortening, butter and
    lard mixed
1 tablespoon ginger

1 tablespoon soda
2 tablespoons warm milk
2 cups bread flour

Heat molasses to boiling point, add shortening, ginger, soda dissolved in warm milk, and flour. Chill thoroughly. Toss one-fourth of mixture on a floured board and roll as thinly as possible; shape with a small round cutter, first dipped in flour. Place near together on a buttered sheet and bake in a moderate oven. Gather up the trimmings and roll with another portion of dough. During rolling, the bowl containing mixture should be kept in a cool place, or it will be necessary to add more flour to dough, which makes cookies hard rather than crisp and short.

Oatmeal Cookies

1 egg
¼ cup sugar
¼ cup thin cream
¼ cup milk

½ cup fine oatmeal
2 cups flour
2 teaspoons baking powder
1 teaspoon salt

Beat egg until light, add sugar, cream, and milk; then add oatmeal, flour, baking powder, and salt, mixed and sifted. Toss on a floured board, roll, cut in shape, and bake in a moderate oven.

Peanut Cookies

2 tablespoons butter
¼ cup sugar
1 egg
1 teaspoon baking powder
¼ teaspoon salt

½ cup flour
2 tablespoons milk
½ cup finely chopped peanuts
½ teaspoon lemon juice

Cream the butter, add sugar, and egg well beaten. Mix and sift baking powder, salt, and flour; add to first mixture; then add milk, peanuts, and lemon juice. Drop from a teaspoon on an unbuttered sheet one-inch apart, and place one-half peanut on top of each. Bake twelve to fifteen minutes in a slow oven. This recipe will make twenty-four cookies.

Cream Sponge Cake

Yolks 4 eggs	1½ teaspoons baking powder
1 cup sugar	¼ teaspoon salt
3 tablespoons cold water	Whites 4 eggs
1½ tablespoons corn-starch	1 teaspoon lemon extract
Flour	

Beat yolks of eggs until thick and lemon-colored, add sugar gradually, and beat two minutes; then add water. Put corn-starch in a cup and fill cup with flour. Mix and sift corn-starch and flour with baking powder and salt, and add to first mixture. When thoroughly mixed add whites of eggs beaten until stiff, and flavoring. Bake thirty minutes in a moderate oven.

Chocolate Cake

3 tablespoons butter
½ cup sugar
1 egg
½ cup milk

1⅓ cups flour
2 teaspoons baking powder
1 square chocolate melted
½ teaspoon vanilla

Cream the butter, add one-half sugar, egg well beaten, and remaining sugar. Mix and sift flour and baking powder, add alternately with milk to first mixture. Then add chocolate and vanilla. Bake thirty minutes in a shallow pan.

Pound Cake

1 lb. butter
1 lb. sugar
Yolks 10 eggs
2 tablespoons brandy

Whites 10 eggs
1 lb. flour
½ teaspoon mace
1 teaspoon baking powder

Cream the butter, add sugar gradually, and continue beating; then add yolks of eggs beaten until thick and lemon colored, whites of eggs beaten until stiff and dry, flour, mace, and brandy. Beat vigorously five minutes. Bake in a deep pan one and one-fourth hours in a slow oven; or if to be used for fancy ornamented cakes, bake thirty to thirty-five minutes in a dripping-pan.

Chocolate Caramels

2½ tablespoons butter   ½ cup milk
2 cups molasses   3 squares chocolate
1 cup brown sugar   1 teaspoon vanilla

Put butter into kettle; when melted, add molasses, sugar, and milk. Stir until sugar is dissolved, and when boiling point is reached, add chocolate, stirring constantly until chocolate is melted. Boil until, when tried in cold water, a firm ball may be formed in the fingers. Add vanilla just after taking from fire. Turn into a buttered pan, cool, and mark in small squares.

HELPFUL HINTS
TO THE YOUNG HOUSEKEEPER

To Scald Milk. Put in top of double boiler, having water boiling in under part. Cover, and let stand on top of range until milk around edge of double boiler has a bead-like appearance.

For Buttered Cracker Crumbs, allow from one-fourth to one-third cup melted butter to each cup of crumbs. Stir lightly with a fork in mixing, that crumbs may be evenly coated and light rather than compact.

To Cream Butter. Put in a bowl and work with a wooden spoon until soft and of creamy consistency. Should buttermilk exude from butter it should be poured off.

To Extract Juice from Onion. Cut a slice from root end of onion, draw back the skin, and press onion on a coarse grater, working with a rotary motion.

To Chop Parsley. Remove leaves from parsley. If parsley is wet, first dry in a towel. Gather parsley between thumb and fingers and press compactly. With a sharp vegetable knife cut through and through. Again gather in fingers and recut, so continuing until parsley is finely cut.

To Caramelize Sugar. Put in a smooth granite saucepan

or omelet pan, place over hot part of range, and stir constantly until melted and of the color of maple syrup. Care must be taken to prevent sugar from adhering to sides of pan or spoon.

To Make Caramel. Continue the caramelization of sugar until syrup is quite brown and a whitish smoke arises from it. Add an equal quantity of boiling water, and simmer until of the consistency of a thick syrup. Of use in coloring soups, sauces, etc.

Acidulated Water is water to which vinegar or lemon juice is added. One tablespoon of the acid is allowed to one quart water.

To Blanch Almonds. Cover Jordan almonds with boiling water and let stand two minutes; drain, put into cold water, and rub off the skins. Dry between towels.

To Shred Almonds. Cut blanched almonds in thin strips lengthwise of the nut.

Macaroon Dust. Dry macaroons pounded and sifted.

To Shell Chestnuts. Cut a half-inch gash on flat sides and put in an omelet pan, allowing one-half teaspoon butter to each cup chestnuts. Shake over range until butter is melted. Put in oven and let stand five minutes. Remove from oven, and with a small knife take off shells. By this method shelling and blanching is accomplished at the same time, as skins adhere to shells.

Flavoring Extracts and Wine should be added if possible to a mixture when cold. If added while mixture is hot, much of the goodness passes off with the steam.

Meat Glaze. Four quarts stock reduced to one cup.

Mixed Mustard. Mix two tablespoons mustard and one teaspoon sugar, add hot water gradually until of the consistency of a thick paste. Vinegar may be used in place of water.

To Prevent Salt from Lumping. Mix with corn-starch, allowing one teaspoon corn-starch to six teaspoons salt.

To Wash Carafes. Half fill with hot soapsuds, to which is added one teaspoon washing soda. Put in newspaper torn in small pieces. Let stand one-half hour, occasionally shaking. Empty, rinse with hot water, drain, wipe outside, and let stand to dry inside.

After Broiling or Frying, if any fat has spattered on range, wipe surface at once with newspaper.

To Remove Fruit Stains. Pour boiling water over stained surface, having it fall from a distance of three feet. This is a much better way than dipping stain in and out of hot water; or wring articles out of cold water and hang out of doors on a frosty night.

To Remove Stains of Claret Wine. As soon as claret is spilt, cover spot with salt. Let stand a few minutes, then rinse in cold water.

To Clean Graniteware where mixtures have been cooked or burned on. Half fill with cold water, add washing soda, heat water gradually to boiling point, then empty, when dish may be easily washed. Pearline or any soap powder may be used in place of washing soda.

To Wash Mirrors and Windows. Rub over with chamois skin wrung out of warm water, then wipe with a piece of dry chamois skin. This method saves much strength.

To Remove White Spots from Furniture. Dip a cloth in hot water nearly to boiling point. Place over spot, remove quickly and rub over spot with a dry cloth. Repeat if spot is not removed. Alcohol or camphor quickly applied may be used.

Tumblers which have contained milk should be first rinsed in cold water before washing in hot water.

To keep a **Sink Drain** free from grease, pour down once a week at night one-half can Babbitt's potash dissolved in one quart water.

Should **Sink Drain** chance to get choked, pour into sink one-fourth pound copperas dissolved in two quarts boiling water. If this is not efficacious, repeat before sending for a plumber.

Never put **Knives** with ivory handles in water. Hot water causes them to crack and discolor.

To prevent **Glassware** from being easily broken, put in a kettle of cold water, heat gradually until water has reached boiling point. Set aside; when water is cold take out glass. This is a most desirable way to toughen lamp chimneys.

To Remove Grease Spots. Cold water and Ivory soap will remove grease spots from cotton and woollen fabrics. Castilian Cream is useful for black woollen goods, but leaves a light ring on delicately colored goods. Ether is always sure and safe to use.

To Remove Iron Rust. Saturate spot with lemon juice, then cover with salt. Let stand in the sun for several hours; or a solution of hydrochloric acid may be used.

Iron Rust may be removed from delicate fabrics by covering spot thickly with cream of tartar, then twisting cloth to keep cream of tartar over spot; put in a saucepan of cold water, and heat water gradually to boiling point.

To Remove Grass Stains from cotton goods, wash in alcohol.

To Remove Ink Stains. Wash in a solution of hydrochloric acid, and rinse in ammonia water. Wet the spot with warm water, put on Sapolio, rub gently between the hands, and generally the spot will disappear.

Cut Glass should be washed and rinsed in water that is not very hot and of same temperature.

In **Sweeping Carpets,** keep broom close to floor and work with the grain of the carpet. Occasionally turn broom that it may wear evenly.

Tie Strands of a New Broom closely together, put into a pail of boiling water, and soak two hours. Dry thoroughly before using.

Never wash the inside of **Tea or Coffee Pots** with soapsuds. If granite or agate ware is used, and becomes badly discolored, nearly fill pot with cold water, add one tablespoon borax, and heat gradually until water reaches the boiling point. Rinse with hot water, wipe, and keep on back of range until perfectly dry.

Never put cogs of a **Dover Egg Beater** in water.

Never wash **Bread Boards** in a sink. Scrub with grain of wood, using a small brush.

Before using a new **Iron Kettle**, grease inside and outside, and let stand forty-eight hours; then wash in hot water in which a large lump of cooking soda has been dissolved.

To clean a **Copper Boiler**, use Putz Pomade Cream. Apply with a woollen cloth when boiler is warm, not hot; then rub off with second woollen cloth and polish with flannel or chamois. If badly tarnished, use oxalic acid. Faucets and brasses are treated in the same way.

A bottle containing **Oxalic Acid** should be marked poison, and kept on a high shelf.

To keep an **Ice Chest** in good condition, wash thoroughly once a week with cold or lukewarm water in which washing soda has been dissolved. If by chance anything is spilt in an ice chest, it should be wiped off at once.

Milk and butter very quickly absorb odors, and if in ice chest with other foods, should be kept closely covered.

Hard Wood Floors and Furniture may be polished by using a small quantity of kerosene oil applied with a woollen cloth, then rubbing with a clean woollen cloth. A very good furniture polish is made by using equal parts linseed oil and turpentine.

Polish for Hard Wood Floors. Use one part bees'-wax to two parts turpentine. Put in saucepan on range, and when wax is dissolved a paste will be formed.

To clean **Piano Keys**, rub over with alcohol.

To remove old **Tea and Coffee Stains**, wet spot with cold water, cover with glycerine, and let stand two or three hours. Then wash with cold water and hard soap. Repeat if necessary.

Before **Sweeping Old Carpets**, sprinkle with pieces of

newspaper wrung out of water. After sweeping, wipe over with a cloth wrung out of a weak solution of ammonia water; which seems to brighten colors.

Platt's Chloride is one of the best **Disinfectants**. Chloride of lime is a valuable disinfectant, and much cheaper than Platt's Chloride.

Listerine is an excellent disinfectant to use for the mouth and throat.

To Make a Pastry Bag. Fold a twelve-inch square of rubber cloth from two opposite corners. Sew edges together, forming a triangular bag. Cut off point to make opening large enough to insert a tin pastry tube. A set comprising bag and twelve adjustable tubes may be bought for two and one-half dollars.

Smoked Ceilings may be cleaned by washing with cloths wrung out of water in which a small piece of washing soda has been dissolved.

For a Burn apply equal parts of white of egg and olive oil mixed together, then cover with a piece of old linen; if applied at once no blister will form. Or apply at once cooking soda then cover with cloth and keep the same wet with cold water. This takes out the pain and prevents blistering.

Curtain and Portière Poles allow the hangings to slip easily if rubbed with hard soap. This is much better than greasing.

Creaking Doors and Drawers should be treated in the same way.

To Remove Dust from Rattan Furniture use a small painter's brush.

SUITABLE COMBINATIONS
FOR SERVING

Breakfast Menus

Oranges
Oatmeal with Sugar and Cream
Broiled Ham   Creamed Potatoes   Pop-overs or Fadges
Coffee

———

Quaker Rolled Oats with Baked Apples, Sugar and Cream
Creamed Fish   Baked Potatoes   Golden Corn Cake
Coffee

———

Bananas
Toasted Wheat with Sugar and Cream
Scrambled Eggs   Sautéd Potatoes   Graham Gems
Griddle Cakes
Coffee

———

Grape Fruit
Wheatlet with Sugar and Cream
Beefsteak   Lyonnaise Potatoes   Twin Mountain Muffins
Coffee

———

Sliced Oranges
Wheat Germ with Sugar and Cream
Warmed over Lamb French Fried Potatoes Raised Biscuits
Buckwheat Cakes with Maple Syrup
Coffee

———

Strawberries
Hominy with Sugar and Cream
Bacon and Fried Eggs   Baked Potatoes   Rye Muffins
Coffee

———

Raspberries
Shredded Wheat Biscuit
Dried Smoked Beef in Cream   Hashed Brown Potatoes
Baking-Powder Biscuit
Coffee

———

Watermelon
Wheat Germ with Sugar and Cream
Broiled Halibut   Potato Cakes   Sliced Cucumbers
Quaker Biscuit
Coffee

———

Canteloupe
Pettijohns with Sugar and Cream
Cecils with Tomato Sauce   Potato Balls   Rice Muffins
Coffee

———

Peaches
Farinose with Sugar and Cream
Omelette   Potatoes à la Maître d' Hôtel   Berry Muffins
Coffee

———

Blackberries
H-O with Sugar and Cream   Dropped Eggs on Toast
Waffles with Maple Syrup
Coffee

———

Pears

Wheatena with Sugar and Cream

Corned Beef Hash   Milk Toast

Coffee

———

Grapes

Cereal with Fruit

Fried Smelts   Baked Sweet Potatoes   Sliced Tomatoes

Oatmeal Muffins

Coffee

———

Oatmeal Mush with Apples

Hamburg Steaks   Creamed Potatoes   White Corn Cake

Coffee

———

Plums and Pears

Cracked Wheat with Sugar and Cream

Baked Beans   Fish Balls   Brown Bread

Coffee

———

Sliced Peaches
Germea with Sugar and Cream   Brown Bread Toast
Cold Sliced Meat   Sautéd Sweet Potatoes
Coffee

Wheatena with Sugar and Cream
Fish Hash   Buttered Graham Toast
Strawberry Short Cake
Coffee

Grapes
Wheat Germ with Sugar and Cream
Lamb Chops   Baked Potatoes   Raised Muffins
Doughnuts and Coffee

Luncheon Menus

Grilled Sardines
Baked Apples with Cream   Rolls   Sponge Cake
Cocoa

Creamed Chicken

Celery   Rolls

Grapes and Apples

Tea

———

Lamb Croquettes

Dressed Lettuce   Baking-Powder Biscuit

Gingerbread   Cheese

Tea

———

Split Pea Soup   Crisp Crackers

Egg Salad   Entire Wheat Bread

Oranges

Cocoa

———

Cold Sliced Meat   Cheese Fondue

Bread and Butter

Sliced Peaches   Cookies

Tea

———

Broiled Ham   Scalloped Potatoes

Brown Bread and Butter

Sliced Oranges   Wafers

———

Scalloped Oysters   Rolls
          Dressed Celery
Polish Tartlets   Tea

———

Salmi of Lamb   Olives
        Bread and Butter
Cake   Chocolate

———

Oyster Stew
Oyster Crackers or Dry Toast
          Pickles
Cream Whips   Lady Fingers

———

Scalloped Turkey
Brown Bread Sandwiches
Lettuce Salad   Cheese Straws
          Tea

———

Turban of Fish   Saratoga Potatoes
      Warmed over Muffins
Nuts   Crackers   Cheese
          Tea

———

Cream of Tomato Soup   Croûtons
          Omelette with Vegetables
            Bread and Butter
Bananas   Tea

———

          Salad à la Russe
       Graham Bread and Butter
Peach Sauce   Scotch Wafers
               Tea

———

          Cold Sliced Tongue
          Macaroni and Cheese
Lettuce Salad   Crackers
     Wafers   Coffee

———

Salmon Croquettes   Rolls
          Dressed Lettuce
       Strawberries and Cream
               Tea

———

       Beef Stew with Dumplings
Sliced Oranges   Cake
               Tea

———

Lobster Salad   Rolls
Raspberries and Cream   Wafers
Russian Tea

———

Cold Sliced Corned Beef
Corn à la Southern
Entire Wheat Bread and Butter
Grapes and Pears

Dinner Menus

Cream of Celery Soup
Roast Beef   Franconia Potatoes   Yorkshire Pudding
Macaroni with Cheese   Tomato and Lettuce Salad
Chocolate Cream
Café Noir

———

Tomato Soup
Baked Fish   Hollandaise Sauce
Shadow Potatoes   Cole Slaw
Fig Pudding
Crackers   Cheese   Café Noir

———

Potato Soup

Boiled Fowl   Egg Sauce   Boiled Rice   Mashed Turnips

Celery   Vegetable Salad

Bread and Butter Pudding

Macaroni Soup

Fricassee of Lamb   Riced Potatoes   Stewed Tomatoes

String Bean and Radish Salad

Fruit and Nuts

Duchess Soup

Fried Fillets of Halibut   Shredded Potatoes   Hot Slaw

Beefsteak Pie

Irish Moss Blanc-Mange with

Vanilla Wafers

Kornlet Soup

Maryland Chicken   Baked Sweet Potatoes

Creamed Cauliflower   Cranberry Sauce

Dressed Lettuce   Polish Tartlets

Café Noir

Vegetable Soup
Veal Cutlets   Horseradish   Mashed Potatoes
Cream of Lima Beans   Dressed Celery
Cerealine Pudding

———

St. Germain Soup
Beefsteak with Oyster Blanket   Stuffed Potatoes   Spinach
Pineapple Pudding   Cream Sponge Cake
Café Noir

———

White Soup
Boiled Salmon   Egg Sauce   Boiled Potatoes   Green Peas
Cucumbers
Strawberries and cream   Cake

———

Tomato Soup without Stock
Braised Beef   Horseradish Sauce   Scalloped Potatoes
Squash
Baked Indian Pudding   Café Noir

———

Bisque Soup
Broiled Shad   Chartreuse Potatoes   Asparagus on Toast
Cucumber and Lettuce Salad
Prune Whip   Custard Sauce

———

Cream of Pea Soup

Boiled Mutton   Caper Sauce   Mashed Potatoes

Turkish Pilaf

Graham Pudding   Fruit and Nuts

———

Turkish Soup

Lamb Chops   French Fried Potatoes   Apple Fritters

Beet Greens

Caramel Custard   Café Noir

———

Irish Stew with Dumplings

Fish Croquettes   Dinner Rolls   Radishes

Custard Soufflé   Creamy Sauce

Crackers   Cheese

———

Black Bean Soup

Halibut à la Créole   Potatoes en Surprise

Brussels Sprouts

Swiss Pudding   Café Noir

———

Cream of Clam Soup

Fried Chicken   Boiled Potatoes

Sliced Tomatoes   Shell Beans

Peach Short Cake   Crackers and Cheese

———

Cream of Lima Bean Soup

Roast Duck   Mashed Sweet Potatoes

Cauliflower au Gratin

Rice Croquettes with Currant Jelly

Grapes   Pears

Crackers   Cheese   Café Noir

———

Chicken Soup

Broiled Sword Fish   Cucumber Sauce

Baked New Potatoes   Sugared Beets

Strawberry Cottage Pudding

Iced Coffee

———

Menu for Thanksgiving Dinner

Oyster Soup   Crisp Crackers

Celery   Salted Almonds

Roast Turkey   Cranberry Jelly

Mashed Potatoes   Onions in Cream   Squash

Chicken Pie

Fruit Pudding   Sterling Sauce

Mince, Apple, and Squash Pie

Neapolitan Ice Cream   Fancy Cakes

Fruit   Nuts and Raisins   Bonbons

Crackers   Cheese   Café Noir

Menu for Christmas Dinner

Consommé   Bread Sticks

Olives   Celery   Salted Pecans

Roast Goose   Potato Stuffing   Apple Sauce

Duchess Potatoes   Cream of Lima Beans

Chicken Croquettes with Green Peas

Dressed Lettuce with Cheese Straws

English Plum Pudding   Brandy Sauce

Frozen Pudding   Assorted Cake   Bonbons

Crackers   Cheese   Café Noir

A Full Course Dinner

FIRST COURSE

Little Neck Clams or Bluepoints, with brown-bread sandwiches. Sometimes canapés are used in place of either. For a gentlemen's dinner, canapés accompanied with sherry wine are frequently served before guests enter the dining-room.

SECOND COURSE

Clear soup, with bread sticks, small rolls, or crisp crackers. Where two soups are served, one may be a cream soup. Cream soups are served with croûtons. Radishes, celery, or olives are passed after the soup. Salted almonds may be passed between any of the courses.

THIRD COURSE
Bouchées or rissoles. The filling to be of light meat.

FOURTH COURSE
Fish, baked, boiled, or fried. Cole slaw, dressed cucumbers, or tomatoes accompany this course; with fried fish potatoes are often served.

FIFTH COURSE
Roast saddle of venison or mutton, spring lamb, or fillet of beef; potatoes and one other vegetable.

SIXTH COURSE
Entrée, made of light meat or fish.

SEVENTH COURSE
A vegetable. Such vegetables as mushrooms, cauliflower, asparagus, artichokes, are served, but not in white sauce.

EIGHTH COURSE
Punch or cheese course. Punch, when served, always precedes the game course.

NINTH COURSE
Game, with vegetable salad, usually lettuce or celery; or cheese sticks may be served with the salad, and game omitted.

TENTH COURSE

Dessert, usually cold.

ELEVENTH COURSE

Frozen dessert and fancy cakes. Bonbons are passed after this course.

TWELFTH COURSE

Crackers, cheese, and café noir. Café noir is frequently served in the drawing and smoking rooms after the dinner.

Where wines and liquors are served, the first course is not usually accompanied by either; but if desired, Sauterne or other white wine may be used.

With soup, serve sherry; with fish, white wine; with game, claret; with roast and other courses, champagne.

After serving café noir in drawing-room, pass pony of brandy for men, sweet liqueur (Chartreuse, Benedictine, or Parfait d'Amour) for women; then Crême de Menthe to all.

After a short time Apollinaris should be passed. White wines and claret should be served cool; sherry should be thoroughly chilled by keeping in ice box. Champagne should be served very cold by allowing it to remain in salt and ice at least one-half hour before dinner time. Claret, as it contains so small an amount of alcohol, is not good the day after opening.

For a simpler dinner, the third, seventh, eighth, and tenth courses, and the game in the ninth course may be omitted.

For a home dinner, it is always desirable to serve for first course a soup; second course, meat or fish, with potatoes and two other vegetables; third course, a vegetable salad, with French dressing; fourth course, dessert; fifth course, crackers, cheese, and café noir.

At a ladies' luncheon the courses are as many as at a small dinner. In winter, grape fruit is sometimes served in place of oysters; in summer, selected strawberries in small Swedish Timbale cases.

Menus for Full Course Dinners

Blue Points

Consommé à la Royal

Olives   Celery   Salted Almonds

Swedish Timbales with Chicken and Mushrooms

Fried Smelts   Sauce Tartare   Dressed Cucumbers

Saddle of Mutton   Currant Jelly Sauce

Potatoes Brabrant   Brussels Sprouts

Suprême of Chicken

Mushrooms à la Sabine

Canton Sherbet

Canvasback Duck   Olive Sauce

Farina Cakes with Jelly

Celery Salad

Apricot and Wine Jelly

Nesselrode Pudding   Rolled Wafers   Parisian Sweets
Crackers   Cheese
Café Noir

———

Little Neck Clams
Consommé au Parmesan
Olives   Salted Pecans
Bouchées
Fillets of Halibut à la Poulette with Mayonnaise
Tomatoes   Delmonico Potatoes   String Beans
Larded Fillet of Beef with Horseradish Sauce
Glazed Sweetbreads
Artichokes with Béchamel Sauce
Sorbet
Broiled Quail with Lettuce and Celery Salad
Bananas   Cantaloupes
Sultana Roll with Claret Sauce
Cinnamon Bars   Lady Fingers   Bonbons
Crackers   Cheese
Café Noir

———

Anchovy Canapés
Julienne Soup
Olives   Celery   Ginger Chips
Oyster and Macaroni Croquettes
Stuffed Fillets of Halibut

French Hollandaise Sauce   Tomato Jelly

Spring Lamb   Potato Fritters

Asparagus Tips with Hollandaise Sauce

Chaud-froid of Chicken

Crême de Menthe Ice

Larded Grouse   Bread Sauce   Lettuce and Radish Salad

Mont Blanc

Bombe Glacée Sponge Drops Almond Crescents Bonbons

Crackers   Cheese

Café Noir

COURSE OF INSTRUCTION

AS GIVEN AT THE

BOSTON COOKING SCHOOL

174 TREMONT STREET

PRACTICE LESSONS

One lesson a week, from 9 to 12.30. Eight Pupils constitute a full class. Pupils may enter one or more classes. After the lesson the food prepared is served to the pupils. Applications to enter classes may be made from October to February. Classes for cooks in Second and Third Courses on Thursday and Friday at 2 P.M.

No extra charge for materials in Cooks' Classes.

FIRST COURSE—Plain Cooking

Twelve Lessons for $12.00. Materials, $3.00.

First Lesson

The Making and Care of a
    Fire
Coffee
Mixing Water Bread
Tomato Soup (without stock)
Croûtons
Boiled Potatoes
Mutton Chops
German Toast

Second Lesson

Baking Bread
Potato Soup
Broiled Fish
Mashed Potatoes
Boiled Eggs
Hash
Scalloped Eggs
Blanc-Mange

Third Lesson

Brown Soup Stock
Mixing Milk Bread
Griddle Cakes
Boiled Fish
Drawn Butter or Egg Sauce
Steamed Potatoes
Tapioca Cream

Fourth Lesson

Vegetable Soup
To Clarify Fat and Try out
    Lard
Baking Milk Bread
Baked Potatoes
Broiled Steak
Broiled Meat Cakes
Baked Custards
Cookies or Ginger Snaps

Fifth Lesson

Beef Stew with Dumplings
Graham Bread
Scalloped Fish
White Sauce
Poached Eggs on Toast
Short Cakes
Gingerbread
Tea

Sixth Lesson

Golden Corn Cake
Fish Balls
Fried Fish
Fried Potatoes
Omelet
Chocolate
Harvard Pudding
Apple and Hard Sauce

Seventh Lesson

Fish Chowder
Stuffed Eggs
Bread Omelet
Bacon
Creamed Potatoes
Graham Gems
Chocolate Bread Pudding
Hard Sauce
Parker House Rolls

Eighth Lesson

Pea Soup
Crisp Crackers
Baked Beans
Veal Cutlets
Doughnuts
Brown Bread
Steamed Squash
Apple Pie

Ninth Lesson

Scotch Broth
Corn Fritters
Tomato Salad
Milk Toast
Sweet Sandwiches
Cake
Eggs in Batter
Sherbet

Tenth Lesson

Roast Beef
Potato Croquettes
Macaroni
Scalloped Cabbage
Cereal with Fruit
Rye Muffins
Prune Pudding
Custard Sauce

Eleventh Lesson

Oyster Soup or Stew
Broiled Oysters
Veal Birds
Cole Slaw
Twin Mountain Muffins
Peach Tapioca Pudding
Coffee Cake
Sandwiches

Twelfth Lesson

Roast or Fricassee Chicken
Rice with Cheese
Creamed Turnips
Hominy Cakes
Plain Lobster
French Dressing
Custard Soufflé
Creamy Sauce

SECOND COURSE—Richer Cooking

Twelve Lessons for $15.00. Materials, $3.00.

First Lesson
Coffee
Baked Apples
Lyonnaise Potatoes
Broiled Beefsteak with Maître
  d'Hôtel Butter
Eggs à la Goldenrod
Rice Griddle Cakes
Soda Biscuit
Frizzled Beef

Second Lesson
Mutton Cutlets Breaded,
  with Tomato Sauce
French Fried Potatoes
Parisienne Potatoes
Baked Eggs
Rye Drop Cakes
Waffles
Lemon Syrup
Chocolate

Third Lesson
Spanish Omelet
Parker House Rolls
Scalloped Oysters
Smothered Oysters
Oysters Sautéd
Eggs in Baskets
Breakfast Bacon
Moulded Snow
Foamy Sauce

Fourth Lesson
Stock for Clear Soup
Broiled Fish
Tartar Sauce
Potato Croquettes
Fish Balls
Macaroni or Spaghetti
Fried Oysters or Scallops
Thanksgiving Pudding
Brandy Sauce

Fifth Lesson

Clear Soup
Egg Balls
Shadow Potatoes
Baked Fish, Sauce
  Hollandaise
Sticks and Rolls
Cabbage Salad
Boiled Dressing
Caramel Custard
Caramel Sauce

Sixth Lesson

Cream of Tomato Soup
Braised Chicken
Potato Balls
Lima Beans
Farina Cakes with Jelly
Raised Muffins
Custard Soufflé
Creamy Sauce
Cold Cabinet Pudding

Seventh Lesson

Purée of Fish
Cusk à la Crême
White Sauce
Curried Lobster
Potato Salad
Apple or Lemon Pie
Cream Cakes
Quaker Bread

Eighth Lesson

Black Bean Soup
Croûtons
Roast Beef
Franconia Potatoes
Yorkshire Pudding
Parsnip Fritters
Spinach
Coffee Cream
Rice Croquettes

Ninth Lesson

Swiss Potato Soup
Stuffed Leg of Mutton
Currant Jelly Sauce
Turkish Pilaf
Turnips in White Sauce
Tea Rolls
Scalloped Apple
Cream Pies

Tenth Lesson

Cream of Celery Soup
Roast Chicken or
Fricassee
Boiled Rice
Cranberry Sauce
Mashed Potatoes
Spider Corn Cake
Cake
Frosting
Snow Pudding

Eleventh Lesson

White Soup
Chicken Croquettes
Broiled Squabs
Apple Fritters
Pinwheel Biscuits
Lady Fingers
Sponge Drops
Charlotte Russe
Orange or
Wine Jelly

Twelfth Lesson

Puff Paste
Oyster Patties
Raspberry Tarts
Creamed Oysters
Lobster Salad
Mayonnaise Dressing
Salted Almonds
Ice Cream or
Sherbet

DINNER COURSE

Twelve Lessons for $18.00. Materials, $6.00.

First Lesson
Oyster Soup
Halibut à la Créole
Chicken Sauté
Creamed Cauliflower
Rolls
Almond Wafers
Orange Trifle
Café Noir

Second Lesson
St. Germain Soup
Broiled Fillet of Beef
Mushroom Sauce
Mashed Sweet Potato
Egg Salad
Fig Pudding
Yellow Sauce
Coffee

Third Lesson
Oyster Gumbo Soup
Baked Fish with Oysters
French Hollandaise Sauce
Hot Slaw
Chicken Salad
Cream Dressing
Chocolate Nougat
Boiled Frosting
Ginger Cream

Fourth Lesson
Purée of Spinach
Lobster Cream
Boned Birds
Creamed Celery
Oysters à la D'Uxelles
Potato Salad
Burnt Almond Charlotte

Fifth Lesson

Bisque of Lobster
Fillet of Beef
Horseradish Sauce
Potatoes au Gratin
Banana Fritters
Shrimp Salad
Pudding à la Macédoine

Sixth Lesson

Potage à la Reine
Puff Paste
Patties
Cream Horns
Cheese Straws
Pineapple Cream

Seventh Lesson

Cream of Asparagus Soup
Lobster à la Newburg
Chicken à la Providence
Chocolate Cream Fritters
Nut Sandwiches
Victoria Punch
Peanut Cookies

Eighth Lesson

Duchess Soup
Halibut à la Poulette
Queen of Muffins
Larded Grouse
Bread Sauce
Ornamental Frosting
Orange Ice

Ninth Lesson

Clam Soup with Poached
  Eggs
Chicken Timbales
Béchamel Sauce
Beefsteak with Oyster
  Blanket
Delmonico Potatoes
Sponge Cake
Baked Alaska

Tenth Lesson

Consommé
Lobster Cutlets
Chicken Soufflé
Mushroom Sauce
Brussels Sprouts
Lemon Queens
Bombe Glacée
Parisian Sweets

Eleventh Lesson	*Twelfth Lesson*
Cream of Lettuce Soup	Cream of Cauliflower Soup
Fillet of Sole	Swedish Timbales
Sauce Tartare	Creamed Sweetbreads
Stewed Mushrooms	Roast Duck
Shredded Potatoes	Olive Sauce
Lobster Salad	Fruit Punch
Marshmallow Cake	Sand Tarts
Café Parfait	Frozen Pudding

SPECIAL LESSONS IN COOKING, by previous appointment, price, $2.00 each. Materials extra.

SPECIAL LESSONS IN LAUNDRY WORK, by previous appointment, price, $2.00 each. Attention given to the doing up of shirts, silk and woollen underwear, colored clothes, table linen, laces, and chiffons.

Afternoon lessons given to Classes in Sick-room Cookery from 2 to 4.30 o'clock. Six lessons for $5.00. Materials, $1.00.

THE NORMAL COURSE extends from January to July. Tuition, $125. For circular and information, apply to the Principal.

DEMONSTRATION LECTURES given during the winter every Wednesday at 10 o'clock A.M. Tickets for course of 12 lectures, with reserved seat, $5.00. Single admission, 50 cents.

DEMONSTRATION LECTURES FOR COOKS, Wednesday and Friday evenings at 7.45 o'clock. Admission, 25 cents.

ROOMS OPEN DAILY, from 9 A.M. to 5 P.M.